DEBI GLIORI is a highly acclaimed author and illustrator
whose previous books for young children include award-winning *Mr Bear* series,
No Matter What and the bestselling *Pure Dead Magic* series.
Her titles for Frances Lincoln include *Amazing Alphabets* and *The Snowchild*.
Debi has five children and lives in Scotland.

for Nina Salkovskis
with lots of love

Little Bear and the Wish Fish copyright © Frances Lincoln Limited 1995
Text and illustrations copyright © Debi Gliori 1995

First published in Great Britain in 1995 by
Frances Lincoln Children's Books, 4 Torriano Mews,
Torriano Avenue, London NW5 2RZ
www.franceslincoln.com

This edition published 2008

British Library Cataloguing in Publication Data available on request

ISBN 978-1-84507-816-4

Set in Garamond Book

Printed in China

9 8 7 6 5 4 3 2 1

Little Bear and the Wish Fish

DEBI GLIORI

F

FRANCES LINCOLN
CHILDREN'S BOOKS

The bears of Papana River Valley led a charmed life.
When it was raining, they fished.
When it was snowing, they hunted.
When the sun shone, they sunbathed.
Life was just peachy.

And yet ... for the bears, the weather was
never quite right.
They complained when it rained, "It's too wet!"
They complained when it snowed, "It's too cold!"
They even complained when the sun came out, "It's too hot!"

The weather-makers were not amused.
The Raindancer, the Sunblazer and the Snowmaker
were doing their best to make perfect weather for bears,
but all they heard in return were loud moans and groans.

So the Raindancer, the Sunblazer
and the Snowmaker decided to teach
those bears a lesson they would
never forget.
First, they caught a fish upstream
of the bear cave.

Next, they gave the fish
the power to grant wishes.
Last of all, they released
the fish, slippety slithery,
back into the river
near the bear cave.

When the bears woke up next morning, they couldn't
see out of their cave for mist.

"Wow!" said Little Bear.

"Where are you, dear?" called Medium Bear.
"You need to wear your rainsuit with five zippers
if you're going out."

"This mist is dismal," moaned Big Bear. "I wish
it would snow."

Straight away, a blizzard began to bombard the valley. The sky turned a grim grey and a gale whipped up the river into ragged, jaggy icebergs.

The Wish Fish hid in a sheltered shallow.

"Wow!" said Little Bear.

"Oh dear," fussed Medium Bear. "Now you need to put on your snowsuit with 40 poppers if you're going out."

"This snow is horrible," moaned Big Bear, "I wish it would be sunny."

Immediately all the snow melted away and the grass was singed brown. The river dried up to a muddy trickle and the Wish Fish flipped and flopped in a puddle outside the bear cave.

"Wow!" shouted Little Bear.

"Now I'm boiling," moaned Big Bear. "I wish I didn't have all this fur."

Oh NO!

"And I'm so sticky," groaned Medium Bear, "I wish we lived in the Arctic Ocean."

Oh GLUB!

"I wish you two would stop moaning and leave me alone," said Little Bear crossly.

Oh HELP!

No sooner said than done.

Little Bear found himself floating all alone in the Arctic Ocean. There was nothing but water and ice all around - not a Medium Bear or Big Bear in sight.

Little Bear was miserable.
  "I'm cold and wet," he moaned.
  "I'm lonely," he moaned.
  "I wish ..."

The Wish Fish surfaced beside him.
"Listen, kid," it said. "Get it right this time,
and no more moaning. One last wish and that's *it*."

Little Bear thought hard.
Waves slapped his muzzle.
He nearly wished that they wouldn't ...
but he stopped himself in time.

The ice froze his head into a furry
popsicle.
He nearly wished for a woolly hat ...
but he stopped himself in time.

Little Bear wasn't a very good swimmer, and his fur was heavy. He began to sink.

He nearly wished for a life-jacket ... Then suddenly he knew what to wish for.

"I wish I lived in a cave by a river
with Big Bear and Medium Bear ...

and weather that snowed sometimes,
rained occasionally,
and was sunny more often than not."

And ... whoosh!

The bears of Papana River Valley
had their charmed life once more.
Big Bear's fur grew back eventually,
Medium Bear decided that the Arctic Ocean
was for polar bears, not cave bears,
and Little Bear taught them both
never to complain again,
because, after all,
life was peachy.

MORE PAPERACKS BY DEBI GLIORI FROM FRANCES LINCOLN CHILDREN'S BOOKS

The Snowchild
Written and illustrated by Debi Gliori

Poor left-out Katie doesn't know how to play.
She has lots of good ideas – but she's always
out of step with the other children's games.
Then, one winter's morning, Katie wakes up
and decides to build a snowman…

ISBN 978-0-7112-0894-0

Amazing Alphabets
Written by Lisa Bruce
Illustrated by Debi Gliori

Not one but eight witty, lively, fun-filled alphabets
for children to enjoy again and again.
Spot the octopus, notice the nutcracker, discover the dragonfly –
learning the alphabet has never been such fun!

978-0-7112-2129-1

Frances Lincoln titles are available from all good bookshops.
You can also buy books and find out more about your favourite titles,
authors and illustrators on our website: www.franceslincoln.com